EARTH MYSTERIES REVEALED

James Bow

Author: James Bow

Editor: Molly Aloian

Project coordinator: Kathy Middleton

Production coordinator: Katherine Berti

Prepress technician: Katherine Berti

Project editor: Tom Jackson

Designer: Paul Myerscough, Calcium Creative

Picture researcher: Clare Newman

Managing editor: Tim Harris

Art director: Jeni Child

Design manager: David Poole

Editorial director: Lindsey Lowe

Children's publisher: Anne O'Daly

Photographs:

Corbis: Bettmann: p. 20 (top)
Istockphoto: front cover; Jolanta Stozek: p. 15 (bottom)
NASA: p. 30; GSFC/METI/ERSDA/JAROS & US and Japan ASTER Science Team: p. 21 (center); Jacques Descloitres, MODIS Rapid Response Team, GSFC: p. 28; JPL/DLR: p. 29 (top); JPL-Caltech/C.Lisse: p. 7
NOAA: p. 26 (bottom)
Photolibrary: Alaska Stock: p. 16 (top)
Science Photo Library: Chris Butler: p. 4–5; Christian Darkin: p. 29 (bottom); Joe Tucciarone: p. 9 (bottom); Detlev Van Ravenswaay: p. 8
Shutterstock: Walter S. Becker: p. 10 (top); Catmando: p. 11; Andrea Danti: p. 10 (bottom); Julien Grondin: p. 19; Amy Nichole Harris: p. 1; Jhaz Photography: p. 14–15; Andreas G. Karelias: p. 12–13; Ralf Juergen Kraft: p. 25; Jason Maehl: p. 27; Navita: p. 14 (bottom); Stijn Peeters: p. 17 (top); Lee Prince: p. 20 (bottom); Reiki Photos: p. 17 (bottom); Kristian Sekulic: p. 22; Silver-John: p. 26 (top); Timage: p. 21 (center)

Illustrations:

BRG: p. 9 (top), 23 (bottom)
Geoff Ward: p. 16 (bottom)

Series created by Brown Reference Group

Library and Archives Canada Cataloguing in Publication

Bow, James, 1972-
Earth mysteries revealed / James Bow.

(Mysteries revealed)
Includes index.
ISBN 978-0-7787-7413-6 (bound).--ISBN 978-0-7787-7428-0 (pbk.)

Earth--Juvenile literature. I. Title.
II. Series: Mysteries revealed (St. Catharines, Ont.)

QB631.4.B69 2010 j550 C2009-906259-3

Library of Congress Cataloging-in-Publication Data

Bow, James.
Earth mysteries revealed / James Bow.
p. cm. -- (Mysteries revealed)
Includes index.
ISBN 978-0-7787-7413-6 (reinforced lib. bdg. : alk. paper)
-- ISBN 978-0-7787-7428-0 (pbk. : alk. paper)
1. Earth sciences--Juvenile literature. 2. Earth--Juvenile literature.
I. Title. II. Series.

QE29.B68 2010
550--dc22

2009042768

Crabtree Publishing Company

www.crabtreebooks.com 1-800-387-7650

In Canada: We acknowledge the financial support of the Government of Canada through the Book Publishing Industry Development Program (BPIDP) for our publishing activities.

Printed in the U.S.A./122009/BG20091103

Published in Canada
Crabtree Publishing
616 Welland Ave.
St. Catharines, Ontario
L2M 5V6

Published in the United States
Crabtree Publishing
PMB 59051
350 Fifth Avenue, 59th Floor
New York, New York 10118

Contents

Introduction

As far as we know, Earth is the only planet with life. However, there are billions of stars in our galaxy alone and who knows how many solar systems. Could Earth be as rare as we think it is?

We take life on Earth for granted, but if Earth had been just a little different, we would not be here. If we were a bit closer to the Sun, our oceans could have boiled away; if we were a bit farther away, there would be nothing but ice and rock. If Earth was a bit smaller, there would be no air to breathe; if it was a little bigger, the **atmosphere** would squash our bodies.

Life support system

So why is Earth the way it is? How did it all begin? What was so special about where, when, and how it formed? What are the forces that are shaping our planet today? Volcanoes and earthquakes create terrible disasters year after year, but without them life would not have started on Earth in the first place.

Planet puzzles

This book investigates the mysteries of planet Earth. Perhaps there is nowhere else like it in the universe...

atmosphere The thin blanket of gases that surrounds a planet or moon

The early Earth was hot, dry, and airless. How has it changed so much?

planet A large round ball of rock, ice, or gas, that moves around a star

How did Earth form from a cloud of dust?

It is believed that the universe began in a Big Bang. At first, there was only clouds of hydrogen and helium atoms. Then the first stars formed.

> **"We are stardust, we are golden, we are billion-year-old carbon."**
> **Joni Mitchell**

Stars use hydrogen and helium as building blocks for heavier **elements**, such as carbon, iron, and oxygen. Once the first stars used up their fuel, they exploded, scattering their contents in huge dust clouds called nebulas.

Making the Sun

Around 4.6 billion years ago, one of those nebulas began to pull itself together. The gravity of all the dust made the cloud shrink. At its center, hydrogen was squeezed into a ball until eventually it burst into light—the Sun was born. Around this new star, the remaining dust and gas began to stick together into larger and larger lumps. Eventually, the cloud had been swept up into the planets—including Earth—and the millions of other objects that make up the solar system.

As the nebula cloud shrunk, it began to spin around. That made all the dust, ice, and gas form into flat rings.

elements Simple substances, such as carbon and iron, that combine to make all things

AMAZING!

The young Earth was a ball of red-hot liquid rock. It took many millions of years for the surface to cool down into solid rock. Even today, planet Earth is **molten** deep inside.

molten Another word for melted

Were the oceans made from rain?

The water in our oceans was originally steam trapped in hot rocks. Over millions of years, steam spewed out of volcanoes, making clouds in the sky. Icy comets crashing into Earth added to the planet's water. Oceans of liquid water could not form until Earth's surface cooled below 212 °F (100 °C). About 3.5 billion years ago, it started to rain—hard. Water collected in the low parts of the planet's surface. However, the ocean was boiled away several times over as the planet was hit by huge **meteorites**. About 3.9 billion years ago, a permanent ocean formed.

Lightning storms electrified the early seas, perhaps sparking off the first life processes.

AMAZING!

A billion years ago, a day on Earth was only 18 hours long. The Moon was closer to Earth then, and Earth spun faster than it does now. Since then, the Moon has drifted away, and our spin has gradually slowed down to once in 24 hours.

meteorites Solid objects from space that have reached Earth's surface

Why is the center of Earth metal?

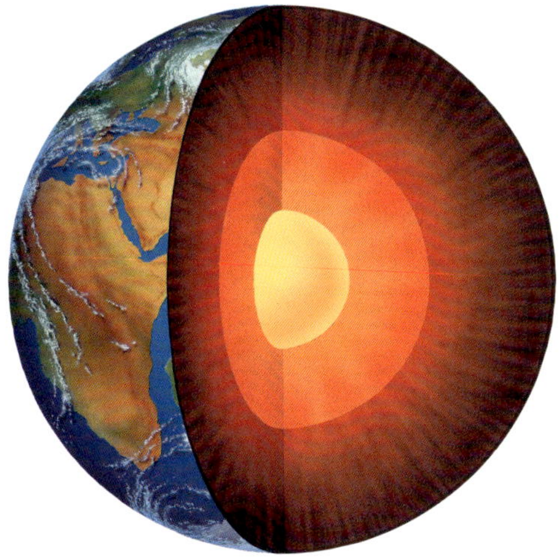

Earth's core is in two parts: the inner core is solid, but the outer core is liquid metal.

As planet Earth formed, the heavier substances, like iron, sunk toward the center. Lighter **minerals** floated up to the surface. The minerals created a thin **crust** of rock, while the metal formed a hot core. However, Earth has more metal—mainly iron—than it should have for its size. How did all of that extra iron get here? Scientists believe that, 4.5 billion years ago, when the Earth was still a molten blob, a Mars-sized planet crashed into Earth. Millions of tons of rock minerals were thrown into **orbit** in an event called the "Big Splash." The Earth absorbed the other planet's core, giving it the extra iron and other heavy metals. The rocks in orbit eventually joined together to become the Moon.

The other planet in the Big Splash is named Thea for the Greek goddess who was the mother of the Moon.

orbit To move around a larger object in space

What makes the northern lights glow?

The Sun is a gigantic nuclear reactor, spewing out heat, light, and stronger **radiation**, known as the solar wind. Earth's metal core makes our planet a giant magnet. The magnetic field shields us from the dangerous solar wind. Near the North Pole, radiation gets close enough to hit Earth's atmosphere, creating the beautiful northern lights.

The scientific name for these lights is aurora.

Earth's magnetism creates a force field around the planet.

SCIENCE EXPLAINED

Earth's core is very hot. It is easily hot enough to melt the metal inside of it. However, the inner core is being squeezed so hard by Earth's weight it has become solid metal. It is still very hot—at least as hot as the surface of the Sun! As the solid part spins around inside the liquid core, it creates a magnetic field. The field bulges out near the poles and curves around through space before going back inside the planet. Magnets in compasses can pick up the field almost anywhere on Earth and show the direction to the poles.

radiation Invisible rays and particles that can be dangerous to life

Where did all the air come from?

As the heavier elements settled to the core of Earth, the lighter elements rose to the top. The lightest of them all were gases, which seeped out of the rocks and formed the atmosphere. At first, Earth's air was made of hydrogen and helium and was very thin. Gradually, gigantic volcanoes released steam, nitrogen, and carbon dioxide, giving Earth a thick atmosphere. Had humans been around we would have choked on this air—there was no oxygen in it. Then, about 3 billion years ago, plant-like bacteria began making oxygen using a process called **photosynthesis**. All the oxygen we breathe today was released from bacteria and plants.

The gases in Earth's early atmosphere came out of volcanoes.

photosynthesis A process used by plants to make food using the energy

Why does the weather always keep changing?

Earth's weather is created by the Sun's heat. But the Sun does not warm the whole planet at the same time.

The Sun's rays beat down at the **tropics** but shine only weakly at the poles. This means the tropics are very hot, but the poles stay cold. Hot air rises, and cold air spreads out near to the ground. That creates currents that are constantly mixing up the air.

> **"The coldest winter I ever spent was a summer in San Francisco."**
> **Mark Twain**

Rain or shine?

Air that flows over oceans tends to pick up **water vapor**, which forms clouds. Over land, the air cools down and dries out. The clouds then drop the water as rain. Land near the ocean has the fastest-changing weather, as hot and cold air rolls in from the sea bringing sunshine, storms, or fog—sometimes all in one day!

A rainbow is created by sunlight shining through raindrops.

tropics Warm parts of the world located near the equator

AMAZING!

Hail is rain that does not fall straight down. Instead, a strong wind inside the cloud blows the raindrops upward. As they rise, the water freezes into balls of ice. Eventually the hailstones are heavy enough to fall back out of the cloud and smash into the ground.

water vapor The gas form of water

What is pushing the wind?

Wind is what you feel when the air blows past you as it moves from one place to another. Air is a mixture of gases such as oxygen and carbon dioxide. Gases are made up of invisible particles, called **molecules**. The molecules whizz around in all directions—and they end up being spread out more or less evenly. The molecules in warm air move faster and are more spread out than those in cold air. When the air in one place gets very spread out—perhaps on a warm day—the gases from colder places rush in to even the differences out. It is going to be a windy day!

Squalls, or sudden gusts of strong wind, are a sign that a rain shower is on the way.

molecules The smallest possible unit of a substance

Where does the electricity in lightning come from?

If you drag your feet across carpet, you might be able to give your friends an electric shock: a little snap, a shock, and maybe even a tiny flash. Lightning is the same thing but on a huge scale. Like your feet on the carpet, air currents rub past each other inside clouds. The rubbing causes loose electrons to move into one part of the cloud and create areas of **charge**. A bolt of lightning is a huge stream of electrons moving between the two areas to even up the difference.

A lightning flash is caused by electrons heating up the air.

SCIENCE EXPLAINED

Electrons are tiny particles inside everything. They have a negative charge. When something has too many electrons it is negatively charged. Something with too few electrons will be positive. Opposite charges attract each other and stick together, like magnets do.

Rubbing a balloon on your head makes hair positively charged. The balloon is negatively charged, so your hair sticks to the balloon.

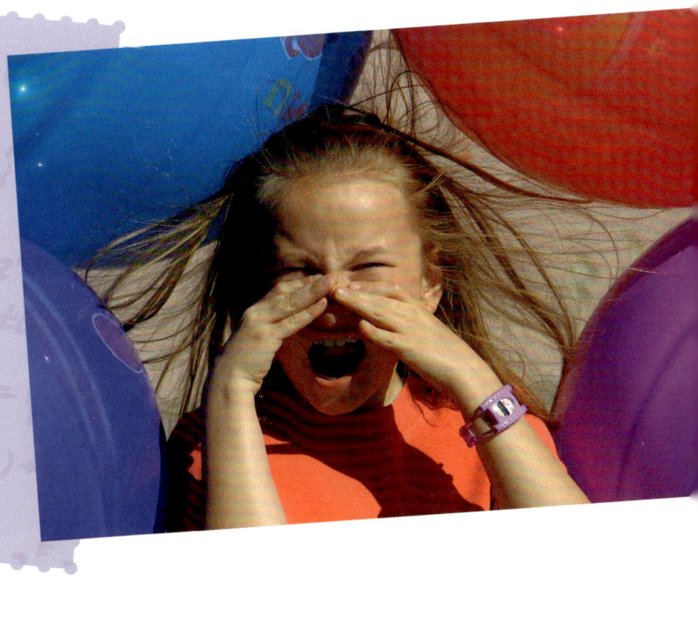

charge A characteristic of a substance; it can be positive, negative, or neutral (no charge)

When the Sun sets in the Arctic winter, it will not rise again for several weeks.

Why is it night all winter long at the North Pole?

Because the Earth is a **sphere**, the Sun's light can shine only on the half of the planet facing the Sun, creating night and day. The line dividing Earth between light and dark is called the terminator. This is where the Sun appears to be rising or setting. As Earth spins, the terminator sweeps around the world every 24 hours. But Earth's **axis** is tilted lightly, so in winter the areas around the poles are always behind the terminator—the Sun never rises. This reverses during the summer when the Sun never sets. This region is often called the Land of the Midnight Sun.

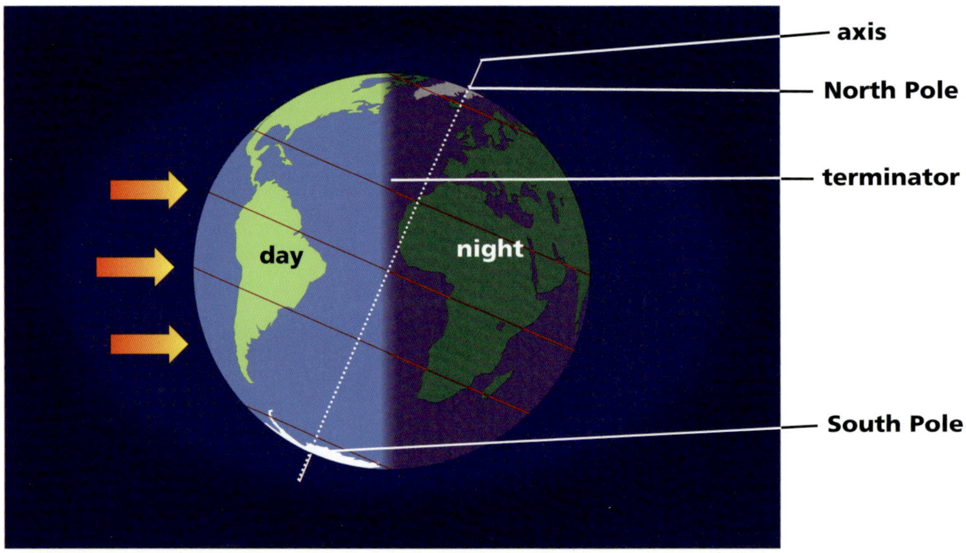

How the Sun's rays light up Earth's surface

axis A line running through the middle of Earth around which the planet spins

Why do sunsets look orange and red?

Shine light through a **prism** and you will see a rainbow on the other side. Prisms refract, or bend, light but each color of light bends by a slightly different amount. Blues bend the most, while reds and oranges bend the least. Earth's atmosphere works like a prism. At sunset, the Sun is shining through a thick layer of air. The air bends the sunlight so we can see it even when the Sun has dropped below the horizon. Blue light is refracted away into the sky, but the red and orange light fills the horizon.

A glass prism bends a beam of light, splitting it into colored rays.

The orange light at dawn and dusk has been refracted from below the horizon.

AMAZING!

Did you know that Earth is actually closer to the Sun in winter? The seasons are not caused by the distance from the Sun, but by the tilt of Earth's axis.

prism A transparent body with a shape that has the effect of bending light

When do volcanoes blow their tops?

Volcanoes release heat from deep inside Earth. The solid crust around the planet is only 20 miles (32 km) deep. Below that is the Earth's mantle, where it is so hot that the rocks melt.

> **"Mountains are produced by volcanoes, and not volcanoes by mountains."**
> **William Hamilton, 1774**

The rocky crust is not a solid sheet. It is actually a series of plates. Thick plates form the land, while thin ones form the seabed. The plates float on the sticky liquid rocks underneath. Volcanoes are located at the gaps between the plates.

Forced out

When the plates are pulling apart, magma, or liquid rock, floods into the crack. Where the plates crash together, they bulge up into mountains. Some mountains are volcanoes. The plates move very slowly, and over many years a bubble of magma builds up under a volcano. Eventually, the force inside gets too strong and the hot rock bursts out!

When magma reaches the surface of Earth, its name changes to lava.

crust The rocky shell covering the surface of Earth

AMAZING!

Surtsey is a very new island near Iceland. It formed in 1963 when a volcano under the sea made a pile of lava. Four years later, Surtsey towered 560 feet (171 m) above sea level. However, since that time, the ocean waves have washed away half the island.

mantle The hot liquid rocks between Earth's core and its crust

How can an earthquake turn dry ground into deadly quicksand?

These apartment buildings have sunk into the ground during an earthquake.

Quicksand is sandy soil containing trapped water. Water pushes between the grains of sand so that, although the ground looks solid, it acts like a liquid. Quicksand forms in swamps or bogs, or around underground streams. An earthquake can also suck water up into dry, sandy soil, creating quicksand. This process is called liquefaction. Buildings that were thought to have been built on solid ground can suddenly sink!

SCIENCE EXPLAINED

Earthquakes occur at faults, or cracks in Earth's surface (left). The rocks on either side of a fault push in opposite directions—sideways or up and down. Sometimes, the rocks get stuck as they grind past each other. Eventually the rocks will crack, and the fault springs apart making the ground around it shake. The result is an earthquake!

AMAZING!

The deadliest earthquake in history was the Shaanxi earthquake in 1556 which killed 830,000 people in China. Most of the dead were killed at home. They lived in caves dug into the hills of soft rocks, which collapsed in the quake.

myth A legend or story that is not true but helps to describe the past

Could the lost city of Atlantis have been destroyed by a volcano?

No one knows if Atlantis ever existed. A **myth** says that it was a great city that was lost beneath the waves. The ancient Greeks thought Atlantis was far to the west. That is where the Atlantic Ocean got its name. However, Atlantis might have been much nearer. About 2,600 years ago, a volcano under the Greek island of Santorini exploded. It blasted a huge crater, which filled up with water and destroyed a city on the island called Akrotiri.

The eruption was the largest ever **witnessed** by humans. Was Akrotiri the real Atlantis?

Today, Santorini is two islands, with a crater in between.

Today, people live on Santorini in beautiful villages on the cliffs around the ancient crater.

witnessed To see and hear something as it actually happened

Why can't I sink in the Dead Sea?

Salty water is **denser** than fresh water. As a result, your body floats slightly better in the ocean than it would in a lake. The Dead Sea between Israel and Jordan has some of the saltiest water in the world. It is so salty that it is impossible to sink under it. The Dead Sea is at the bottom of the deepest hole anywhere on Earth's surface. Water flowing in from rivers and streams carries a little bit of salt with it. Once it reaches the sea, the water slowly **evaporates** in the desert sunshine. But the salts stay in the sea, making it saltier and saltier. The Dead Sea is ten times saltier than the ocean.

Swimmers can float in the Dead Sea without having to paddle at all.

denser To have more material squeezed inside than another substance

Why is the Atlantic Ocean getting wider?

The floor of the Atlantic Ocean is split in two. Running down the center is a line of undersea mountains and deep valleys called the Mid-Atlantic Ridge. Molten rock rises up as this split widens, cooling to form new ocean floor. North America drifts an inch (2.5 cm) away from Europe and Africa each year. Meanwhile, the Pacific Ocean is getting smaller. North and South America drift west as the Atlantic Ocean widens, running over the top of the plates of the Pacific. Where they collide, the edges of the different plates under the Pacific Ocean are pushed into the mantle. The two American plates are forced up into the Rocky and Andes mountains.

The movements of plates is powered by currents flowing through the magma.

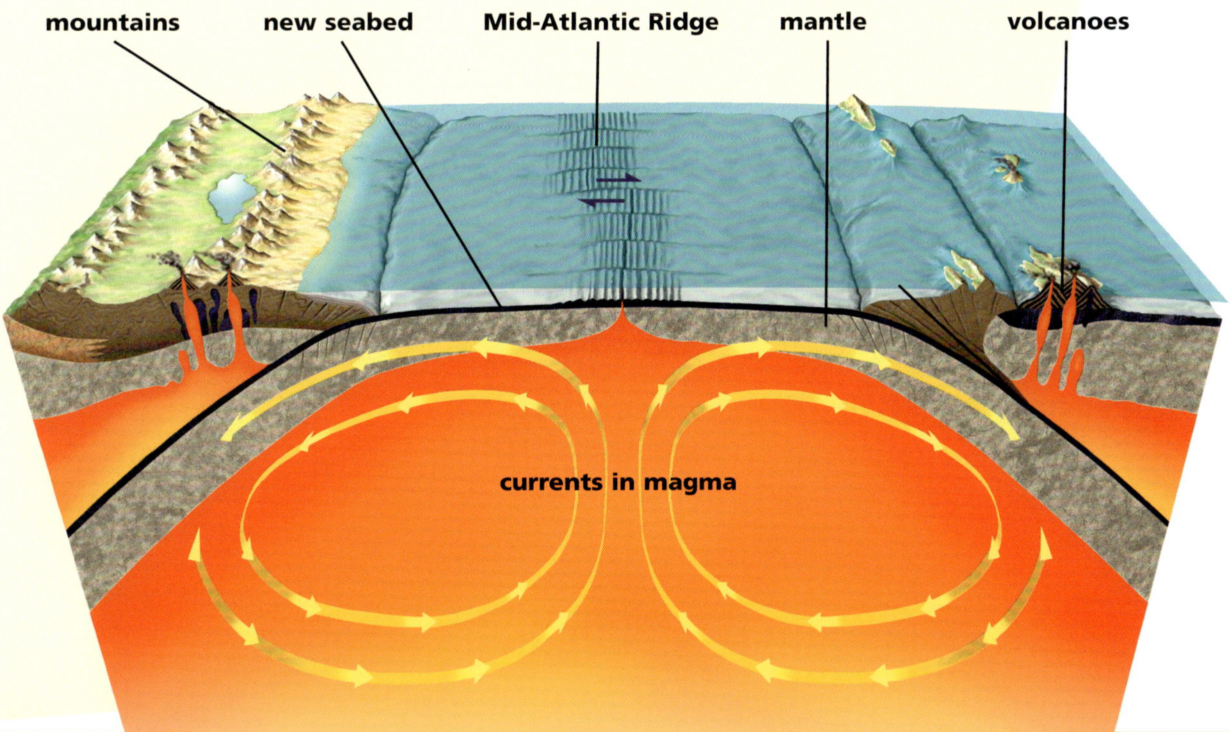

evaporates To turn from a liquid into a gas

What makes Earth the only planet with life?

We are in exactly the right place. We exist in a "Goldilocks orbit," not too hot that our oceans boil, and not too cold that they freeze.

Earth is also just the right size to have a thick atmosphere, but not so big that we are crushed by our gravity. The iron in our core produces a magnetic field that shields us from the worst of the Sun's radiation. Even the Moon helps, producing tides that shake up the ocean, stirring up **nutrients** used by living things. But the most important factor is water. Most plants and animals contain water and use it to release **energy** from food. Water also keeps our weather stable. When looking for other planets that might support life, scientists look for water.

> **"Earth is like a spaceship that didn't come with an operating manual."**
>
> **Buckminster Fuller**

Earth is the third of eight planets in the solar system.

nutrients The chemicals needed by living things to grow

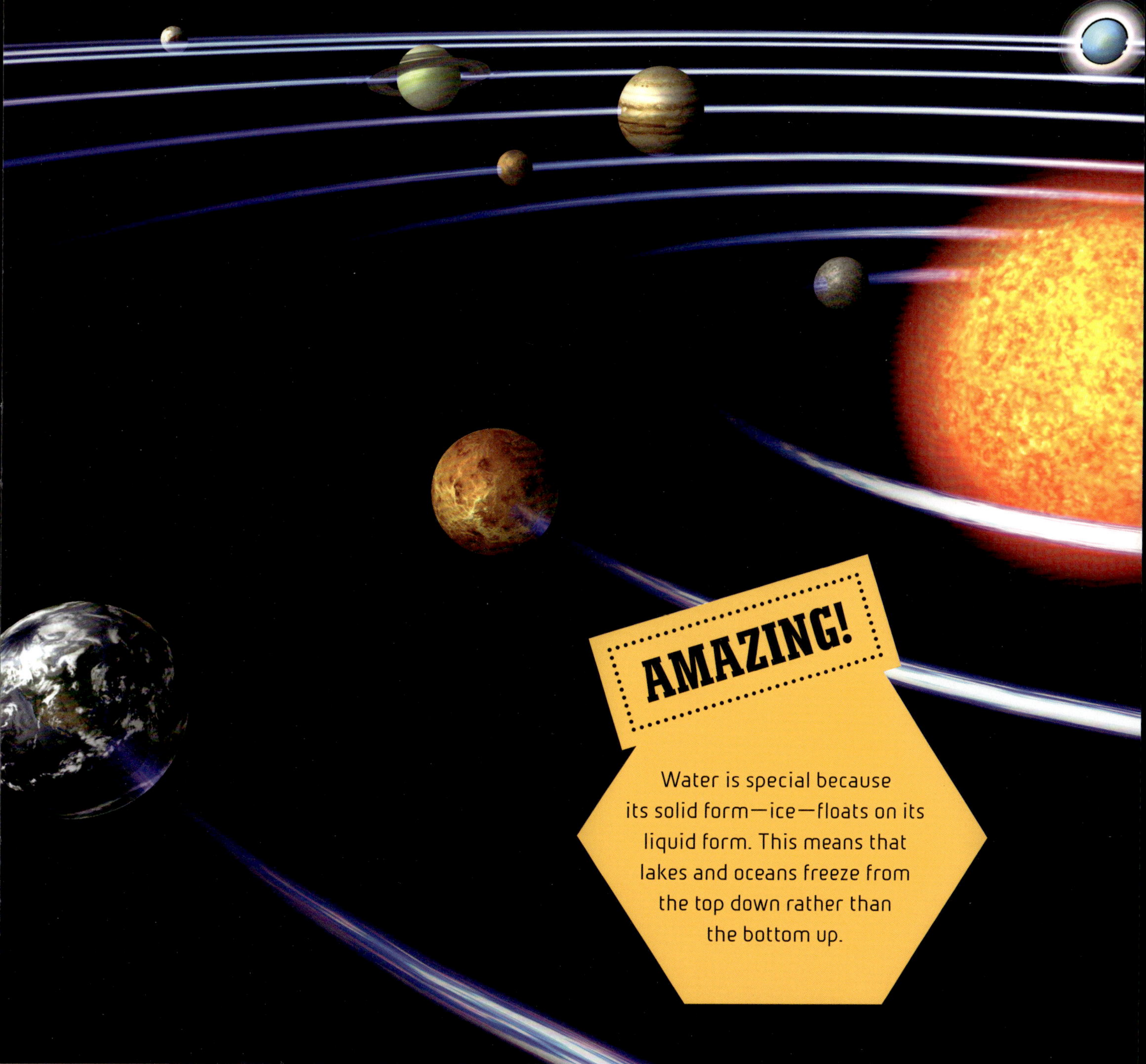

AMAZING!

Water is special because its solid form—ice—floats on its liquid form. This means that lakes and oceans freeze from the top down rather than the bottom up.

energy The power required to move and survive

How is life on Earth fueled by the Sun?

Animals survive by eating plants—or perhaps other animals. Plants and many bacteria do not eat. Instead they trap the energy from the Sun's light and use it to turn water from the soil and carbon dioxide in the air into sugar. The process is photosynthesis, and the sugar made by it is the fuel for almost all life on Earth. When you eat an apple or drink some orange juice, the sweet sugar in it was made using sunlight.

Leaves look green because a plant absorbs the red and blue light to power its photosynthesis.

SCIENCE EXPLAINED

Not all living things rely on the Sun's energy to survive. A few creatures can live without the Sun. Creatures living around black smokers, or hot springs on the ocean floor, take their energy from the heat coming from Earth's mantle. The smokers pump out water filled with nutrients, which bacteria can use for fuel. Everything else in the area survives thanks to the bacteria. For example, deep-sea tubeworms have bacteria living inside their bodies.

Black smokers are found near midocean ridges.

absorbs Takes in

The colors in this spring are created by bacteria living on the chemicals in the hot water.

How do bacteria live in deep rocks?

Endoliths and hypoliths are bacteria that live in the tiny spaces inside rocks. They get in through cracks or dig their way in. The rock bacteria feed on tiny amounts of chemicals, such as iron, potassium, and sulfur, inside. Endoliths and hypoliths are extremophiles—**microbes** that live in extreme conditions that would kill other life.

microbes Tiny life-forms that are too small to see without a microscope

The Great Barrier Reef near Australia can be seen from orbit.

What living things can you see from space?

It depends on how close you are. From Mars, Earth appears as a bright blue point of light in the night sky. However, in Earth's orbit, you can see forests, coral reefs, and grasslands. Signs of **civilization** are also easy to see, including pyramids in Egypt, airports, and highways. But how can we see if there is life on other planets? Looking at their atmosphere can give us clues. Mars has **methane** in its air. The methane on Earth is made by living things. What made Mars's methane?

AMAZING!

Earth is being bombarded by stuff from space all the time. About 100 tons (90 metric tons) of space rock lands on Earth's surface every day. Luckily, nearly all of the rock is fine, powdery dust—not huge fireballs of rock.

civilization The environment of houses and cities that humans build for themselves

Where else in the solar system might life exist?

Extremophiles might be able to survive in the most extreme environment of all—another planet. However, life still needs liquid water and a source of energy. Scientists are looking at Jupiter's ice moon, Europa, which may have an ocean of liquid water under the surface.

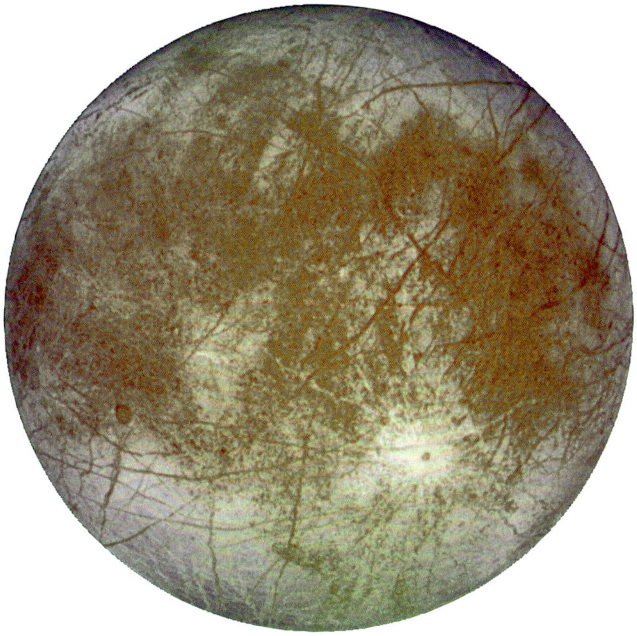

The surface of Europa is solid ice covered in cracks and volcanoes that erupt steam, not lava!

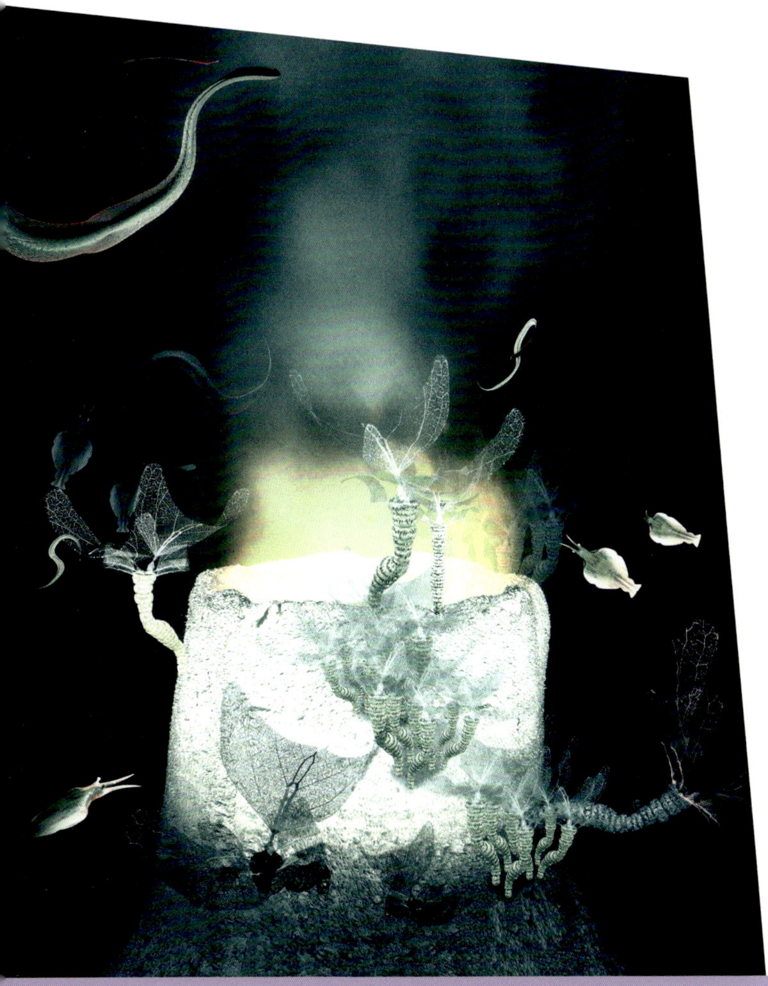

Scientists are also looking at Mars for life. This planet may have had oceans billions of years ago—and perhaps simple life. If we find fossils of life on Mars, it would mean that there is probably life elsewhere in the universe. And, if water still exists on Mars, perhaps life is there, too.

It is possible that aliens live around hot springs at the bottom of Europa's oceans.

methane A kind of gas made from carbon and hydrogen

Earth Facts

The distance around the equator is 42 miles (67 km) longer than the distance around the Earth over the poles.

Even though Mount Everest is the world's tallest mountain, the top of Ecuador's Mount Chimborazo is furthest from the center of the Earth.

The air pressure in a hurricane is so low that the surface of an ocean is sucked upward by the storm, raising the sea level by several feet.

Find Out More

Books

Shaky Ground: Earthquakes by Mary Colson. Raintree, 2006.

Weather Watcher by John Woodward. DK Publishing, 2006.

Destination Earth by Tom Jackson. PowerKids Press, 2010.

Web Sites

National Geographic Volcanoes
http://video.nationalgeographic.com/video/player/environment/environment-natural-disasters/volcanoes/volcano-eruptions.html

World Sunlight Map
www.die.net/earth/

How Hurricanes Work
www.howstuffworks.com/hurricane.htm

Glossary

absorbs Takes in

atmosphere The thin blanket of gases that surrounds a planet or moon

axis A line running through the middle of Earth around which the planet spins

charge A characteristic of a substance, it can be positive, negative, or neutral (no charge)

civilization The environment of houses and cities that humans build for themselves

crust The rocky shell covering the surface of Earth

denser To have more material squeezed inside than another substance

elements Simple substances, such as carbon and iron, that combine to make all things

energy The power required to move and survive

evaporates To turn from a liquid into a gas

mantle The hot liquid rocks between Earth's core and its crust

meteorites Solid objects from space that have reached Earth's surface

methane A kind of gas made from carbon and hydrogen

microbes Tiny life-forms that are too small to see without a microscope

minerals Crystals and other substances that make up different types of rocks

molecules The smallest possible unit of a substance

molten Another word for melted

myth A legend or story that is not true but helps to describe the past

nutrients The chemicals needed by living things to grow

orbit To move around a larger object in space

photosynthesis A process used by plants to make food using the energy in sunlight

planet A large round ball of rock, ice, or gas, that moves around a star

prism A transparent body with a shape that has the effect of bending light

radiation Invisible rays and particles that can be dangerous to life

sphere A round shape, like a soccer ball

tropics Warm parts of the world located near the equator

water vapor The gas form of water

witnessed To see and hear as something actually happened

Index